A Christmas Story

Brian Wildsmith

EERDMANS BOOKS FOR YOUNG READERS
GRAND RAPIDS, MICHIGAN / CAMBRIDGE, U.K.

Once, a long time ago in a town called Nazareth,
a little donkey was born.

When the little donkey was almost nine months old, his mother set
out on a long trip with her mistress and master, whose names were

Mary and Joseph. They asked Rebecca, a child who lived nearby, to look after the little donkey while they were gone.

But the little donkey was very sad without his mother and refused to eat. So Rebecca packed food and water and promised the little donkey that they would find his mother.

And they set out to follow Mary and Joseph.

The roads were full of people traveling to various towns and cities.
"Have you seen a donkey with a man and a woman?" Rebecca
asked a traveler.
"Yes, they passed me on the road to Jerusalem," the traveler replied.

Rebecca and the little donkey took the road to Jerusalem. Soon they came to a soldier standing guard at a splendid palace.

"Have you seen a donkey with a man and a woman?" Rebecca asked the soldier.

"Yes, they passed this way," the soldier answered. "Now hurry along. There are important visitors here to see King Herod."

Rebecca and the little donkey continued on their way. In time, they
met some shepherds keeping watch over their flocks.

"Have you seen a donkey with a man and a woman?" Rebecca asked them.

"Yes, they were going toward Bethlehem," the shepherds replied.

So the little donkey and Rebecca went on. Suddenly glorious music filled the sky. And then they saw a great star shining down on the little town of Bethlehem.

When they reached Bethlehem, they met a man
standing in the doorway of an inn. Rebecca asked if he had
seen Mary and Joseph and the donkey.

"Yes," he replied. "They wanted to stay here, but there
was no room at the inn. They went to the stable." And the
innkeeper showed Rebecca the way.

The stable was bathed in a wonderful light that shone from the bright star above.

As Rebecca and the little donkey came near, they heard the sweet sounds of a mother donkey braying and a little baby crying.

Rebecca and the little donkey entered the stable. And there, lying in a manger, was a newborn baby.

"What are you going to call him?" asked Rebecca.
"His name is Jesus," Mary replied.

In the days that followed, the little donkey and his mother
went with Mary and Joseph and the baby Jesus into Egypt. And
Rebecca rode home on a king's camel.

And it came to pass that Mary and Joseph returned to
Nazareth, and there Jesus grew up, with Rebecca as his friend.

For Little Ornella

This edition of *A Christmas Story,*
originally published in English in 1989,
is published by arrangement with
Oxford University Press.

This edition published in 1998 in
the United States by
Eerdmans Books for Young Readers
an imprint of Wm. B. Eerdmans Publishing Co.
255 Jefferson Ave. S.E.,
Grand Rapids, Michigan 49503
P.O. Box 163, Cambridge CB3 9PU U.K.

Printed in Hong Kong

03 02 01 00 99   7 6 5 4 3 2

Library of Congress Cataloging-in-Publication Data
Wildsmith, Brian.
A Christmas story / written and illustrated by Brian Wildsmith.
p.   cm.
Summary: Rebecca, a young girl living in Nazareth, accompanies a
small donkey searching for his mother to a stable in Bethlehem, where they
both witness a special event.
ISBN 0-8028-5173-8 (cloth: alk. paper)
1. Jesus Christ — Nativity — Juvenile fiction. [1. Jesus Christ — Nativity — Fiction.
2. Donkeys — Fiction. 3. Christmas — Fiction.] I. Title.
PZ7.W647Ch 1998
[E] — dc21   98-18067
                                                                CIP
                                                                AC